Sticky

TITCH

Pat Hutchins

RED FOX

A Red Fox Book

Published by Random House Children's Books
20 Vauxhall Bridge Road, London SW1V 2SA

A division of The Random House Group Ltd
London Melbourne Sydney Auckland
Johannesburg and agencies throughout the world

Copyright © Pat Hutchins 2000
Copyright © photographs Hutchins Film Company Limited

A Hutchins Film Company Limited production for Yorkshire Television

1 3 5 7 9 10 8 6 4 2

First published by Red Fox 2000

Printed and bound in Hong Kong.

THE RANDOM HOUSE GROUP Limited Reg. No. 954009

ISBN 0 09 940014 6

Dad was very excited. He'd just got a ticket for the Cup Final.

He was so pleased, he said that Titch could help him fix some loose tiles in the kitchen.

'But be careful, Titch,' said Dad. 'I've just put glue on the floor. Don't stand on it.'

Oh dear! Too late! Titch had put his foot on the sticky floor. He had to pull really hard to free his foot.

When he'd finished helping Dad, Titch went upstairs
to see what Peter and Mary were doing.
His foot felt a bit sticky.

Mary was about to glue some cards into her scrapbook.

'Can I stick some in for you?' asked Titch.
'No,' said Mary, jumping up. 'You're not very good at sticking things in scrapbooks.'

But as Mary jumped up, all the loose cards fell to the floor.

Then Titch went into Peter's room.

Peter was about to stick some stamps into his stamp album.

'Can I stick some in for you?' asked Titch.

But as Titch leaned on the album, all the stamps fell to the floor.

Then Titch went downstairs
to see if Dad needed
any more help.

Dad was shouting from the kitchen. He'd lost his ticket to the Cup Final!

Where could it be?

Titch decided to ask Peter and Mary if they had seen Dad's ticket.

Now Mary was making a fuss.

She'd lost her favourite card, and she wanted to stick it in her album. Where could that card have got to?

Now Peter was making a fuss, too. Titch decided to
see what was wrong.

He couldn't find his best stamp to put in the album!
  Where could it be?

Downstairs, Dad was still looking for his ticket.

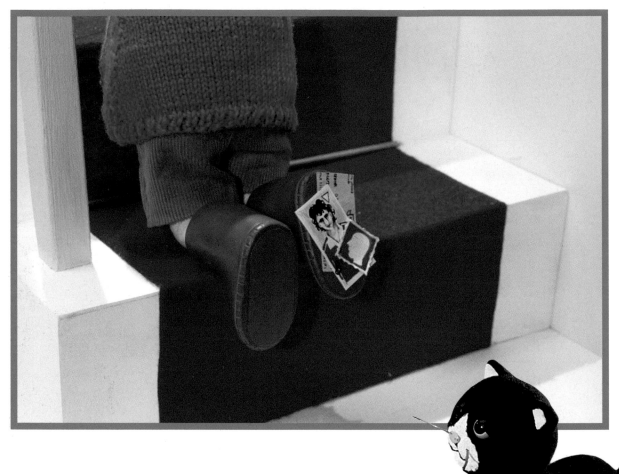

But look!
   The ticket and the card and the stamp had all stuck to Titch's sticky foot! He must have trodden on them!

'I've found them,' said Titch.

'I'm glad you found my favourite card,' said Mary.

'I'm glad you found my best stamp,' said Peter.

'And I'm very glad you found my Cup Final ticket,' said Dad.

'Well done, Titch!' said Mum.